The Animals' Ark

MARIANNE DUBUC

Kids Can Press

Pip! Pop!

It had begun to rain in the animal kingdom.
Lightly at first, and then —

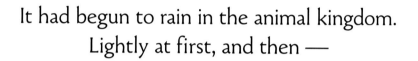

Pip! Pop! Pip! Pop! Pip!
Pip! Pop! Pip! Pop! Pip!
Pip! Pop! Pip! Pop! Pip!
Pip! Pop! Pip! Pop! Pip!

It began to pour!
There was so much water everywhere,
the animals didn't know where to seek shelter.

Then a funny-looking sea creature
appeared on the horizon ...

Was it a whale?

Or an octopus?

No — it was a boat,
and a kindly man inviting
the animals aboard!

Two by two,
the animals stepped aboard,
careful not to tread on
any paws or tails.

There had never been so many
animals on one boat before!

At first, things were a little hurly-burly.

But everyone quickly found a spot.

Outside, it seemed the rain wouldn't ever stop.

Below deck, the animals settled in.

The birds made their nest ...

and the sheep played leapfrog.

The crocodile had his teeth cleaned ...

and the ladybugs played dominoes.

Some of the animals were
terribly bored,
but others had a
grand time!

1... 2... 3...

And all the while, the rain fell.

The zebra counted her stripes ...

and the elephants swung.

The goldfish didn't quite know
what to do with himself ...

and the cat was feeling peckish.

Suddenly, a **storm** swelled.

The ship was tossed about on the waves.

Howling and crashing,
the storm lasted for several days.

The animals were beside themselves.

Then one morning, though the rain still fell,
the sea finally calmed.

What a **relief!**

The animals went back to their activities.
The tiger enjoyed a nap ...

while the chameleon played hide-and-seek.

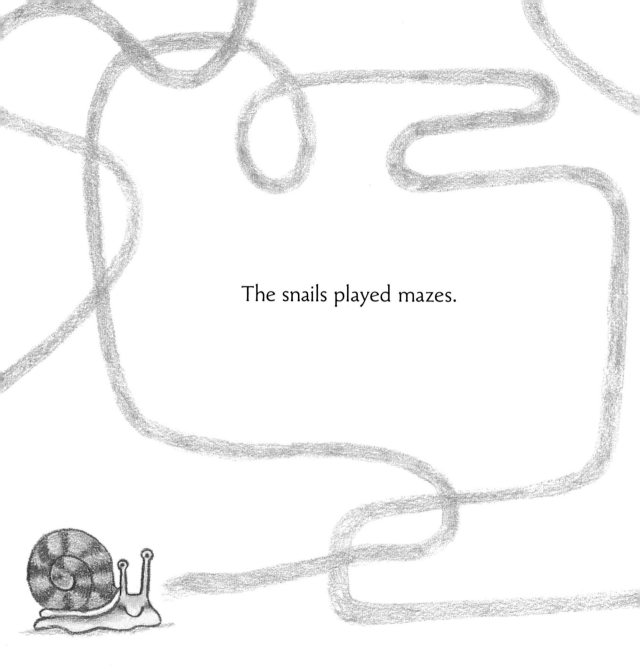

The snails played mazes.

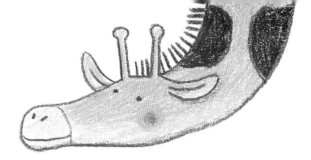

The mouse,
the cat,
the turtle
and
the giraffe
had
a contest
to see
who
was
tallest.

But before the winner was announced,
the ship sprang a leak!
What terrible luck!

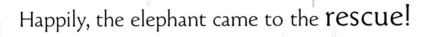

Happily, the elephant came to the rescue!

Through the rain, the boat sailed on.
The animals **couldn't wait**
to set paw on dry land.

The penguins were overheating ...

and the rabbits were seasick.

The rhinos took up
**too much
room ...**

the hedgehogs were a
thorn in others' hides ...

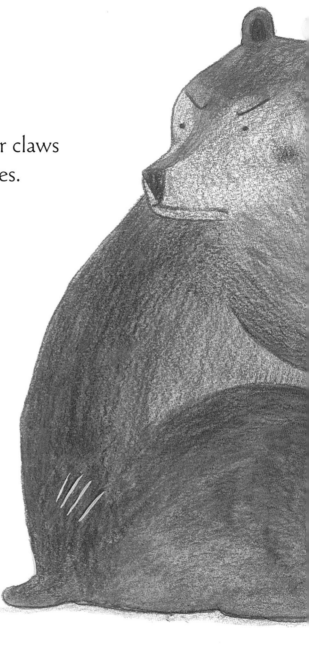

and the cat sharpened her claws
in all the wrong places.

Tired of the quarreling, one of the birds flew off
in search of land ...

Things aboard the ship were in shambles.

The animals were
very discouraged.

Still the rain fell, **day** and **night**.

Until at last one evening, the clouds gave way
to a magnificent starry sky.

And the little bird returned with good news:

She had found a spot where the animals
could make a new home.

Hooray!

The crew set a course to follow
their feathered friend.

They followed the little bird for several days,
and then one morning ...

the giraffe shouted: "Land, ho!"

At last, the animals disembarked the boat
that had saved them from the flood.

"Goodbye and **thank you,** Mr. Noah!"

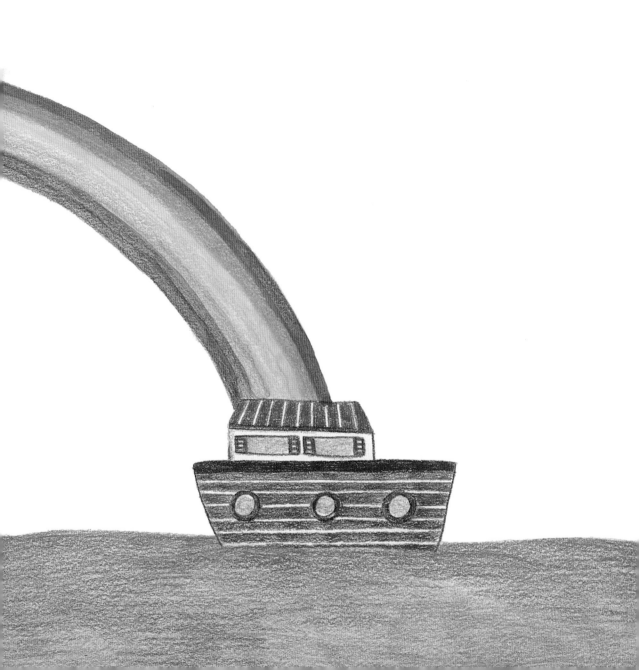

First written in French under the title *L'arche des animaux.*

Text and illustrations © 2015 Marianne Dubuc
Translation rights arranged through VeroK Agency, Spain
English translation © 2016 Kids Can Press

Kids Can Press acknowledges the financial support of the Government of Ontario,
through the Ontario Media Development Corporation's Ontario Book Initiative; the Ontario
Arts Council; the Canada Council for the Arts; and the Government of Canada,
through the CBF, for our publishing activity.

Published in Canada by
Kids Can Press Ltd.
25 Dockside Drive
Toronto, ON M5A 0B5

Published in the U.S. by
Kids Can Press Ltd.
2250 Military Road
Tonawanda, NY 14150

www.kidscanpress.com

The artwork in this book was rendered in pencil crayon.
The text is set in Paradigm Light.

English edition edited by Yvette Ghione
English edition designed by Marie Bartholomew

This book is smyth sewn casebound.
Manufactured in Malaysia in 10/2015 by Tien Wah Press (Pte.) Ltd.

CM 16 0 9 8 7 6 5 4 3 2 1

Library and Archives Canada Cataloguing in Publication

Dubuc, Marianne, 1980–
[Arche des animaux. English]
The animals' ark / Marianne Dubuc.

Translation of: L'arche des animaux.
ISBN 978-1-77138-623-4 (bound)

I. Title. II. Title: Arche des animaux. English.

PS8607.U2245A7313 2016   jC843'.6   C2015-904681-5

Kids Can Press is a *Corus*™ Entertainment company